FIREFLIES FOR NATHAN

Fireflies
FOR NATHAN

SHULAMITH LEVEY OPPENHEIM

pictures by JOHN WARD

TAMBOURINE BOOKS NEW YORK

For Nathan and Jonas, with love
S.L.O.

To the memory of Lessie Ward Smitherman, my nana,
and to Gladys Lee, my grandma
J.W.

Text copyright © 1994 by Shulamith Levey Oppenheim. Illustrations copyright © 1994 by John Ward.
All rights reserved. No part of this book may be reproduced or utilized in any form or by any means, electronic or mechanical, including photocopying, recording, or by any information storage or retrieval system, without permission in writing from the Publisher. Inquiries should be addressed to Tambourine Books, a division of William Morrow & Company, Inc., 1350 Avenue of the Americas, New York, New York 10019. Printed in the United States of America. Book design by Filomena Tuosto. The text type is Bitstream Matt Antique. The illustrations were painted with acrylic on canvas.

Library of Congress Cataloging in Publication Data
Oppenheim, Shulamith Levey. Fireflies for Nathan/by Shulamith Levey Oppenheim; illustrated by John Ward. –1st ed. p. cm. Summary: With the help of his grandparents, six-year-old Nathan catches fireflies and keeps them in a jar by his bed, just as his father did when he was six. [1. Fireflies–Fiction. 2. Grandparents–Fiction.] I. Ward, John (John Clarence), ill. II. Title. PZ7.0618Fi 1994 [E]–dc20 93-29568 CIP AC
ISBN 0-688-12147-O (trade). –ISBN 0-688-12148-9 (lib. bdg.)
1 3 5 7 9 10 8 6 4 2
First edition

Nathan asks,
"When Daddy lived here, was he little like me?"
Nana smiles. "He was.
We came here when he was almost six."

"I'm six already," Nathan says.

"You are," and Nana kisses Nathan on the cheek.

"What was Daddy's favorite thing to do
when he was six?" Nathan asks.

Nana thinks and thinks.

"Fireflies," she says.

"When night came on, the three of us—your poppy, too—
would creep across the lawn
just when the fireflies began to star the grass.
Your daddy caught a few—three, four, or five.
Enough to make a shining lamp.
I know exactly where the jar has been."

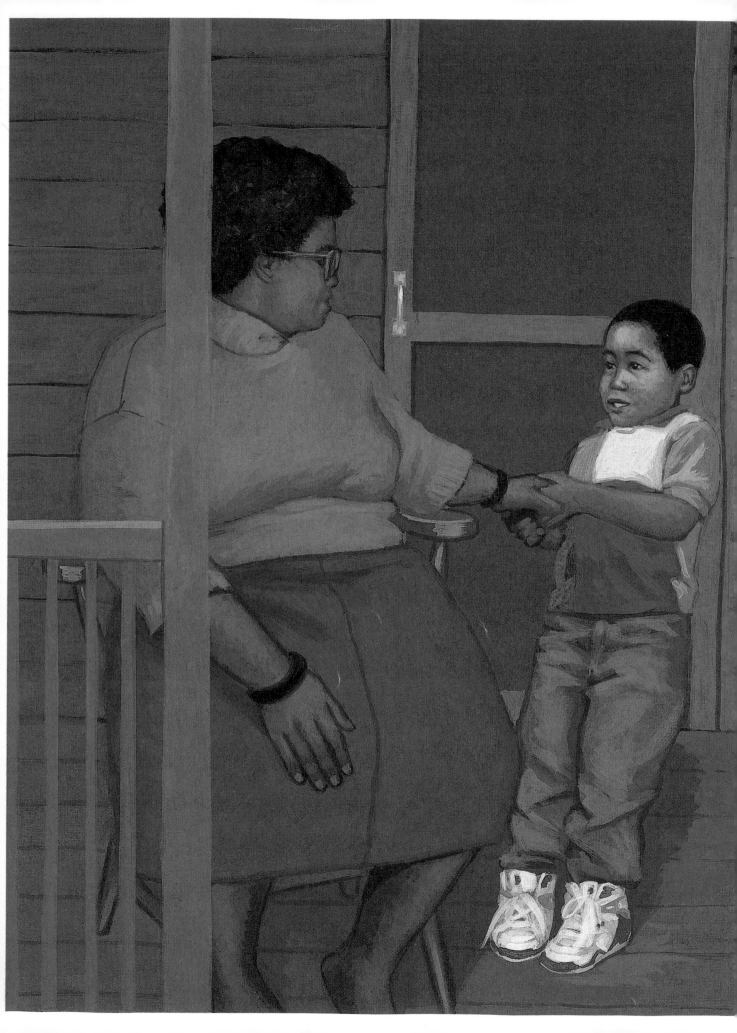

Nathan jumps up.
"Please, Nana, let's go in and get the jar.
It's almost night."

Nathan and Nana and Poppy are sitting in the grass.
The sky is streaked with red.
They're waiting for the night to come.
Their feet are bare.

A ladybug begins a journey over Nathan's toes.
A goldfinch lights atop a spread of Queen Anne's lace.
A monarch butterfly wings in and out.
Deep in the pond the bullfrogs croak
Good Night, Good Night.

The minutes pass.
Nathan shakes his leg.
The ladybug falls off his foot.
He tugs at Poppy's sleeve.
"Not yet," Poppy says.

More minutes pass.
Nathan pulls at Nana's arm.
"It's getting dark.
Where are the fireflies, Nana?"
"They'll be here soon."
Nana and Poppy nod their heads.

And *very* soon
one, two, then three and four,
the firefly glows appear.
The blinking yellow lights are everywhere
above the grass.

Nathan and Nana and Poppy creep across the lawn.
"Slowly, slowly," Poppy whispers.
"Let Nana hold the jar."

Nathan cups his hands around a glow.
"I've got one, Poppy!
Nana, I want to see it blinking on and off."
"Careful," Nana warns.

But it's too late.
The firefly is gone.
Nana whispers, "Just like your daddy.

"You have to keep your hands cupped tightly
till you drop the firefly in the jar."
Nathan promises, "I will," and soon
the jar becomes a beacon in the night.

The firefly jar is sitting by the bed.
Nana tucks the sheet up under Nathan's chin.
Poppy kisses Nathan's cheek.
"Do you like catching fireflies with me?" Nathan asks.
"We do."
"Just as much as with my daddy?"
"Just as much."
"You can let them out when I'm asleep."
Nana and Poppy smile.
"That's what your daddy always said."

"I'm going to tell Mommy and Daddy all about catching fireflies with you."
Nathan yawns and lays the firefly jar beside him on the pillow.
He presses his cheek against the glass.
"Nana, I'm glad you saved the jar."
"And so are we," Nana and Poppy tiptoe from the room.
"And so are we."

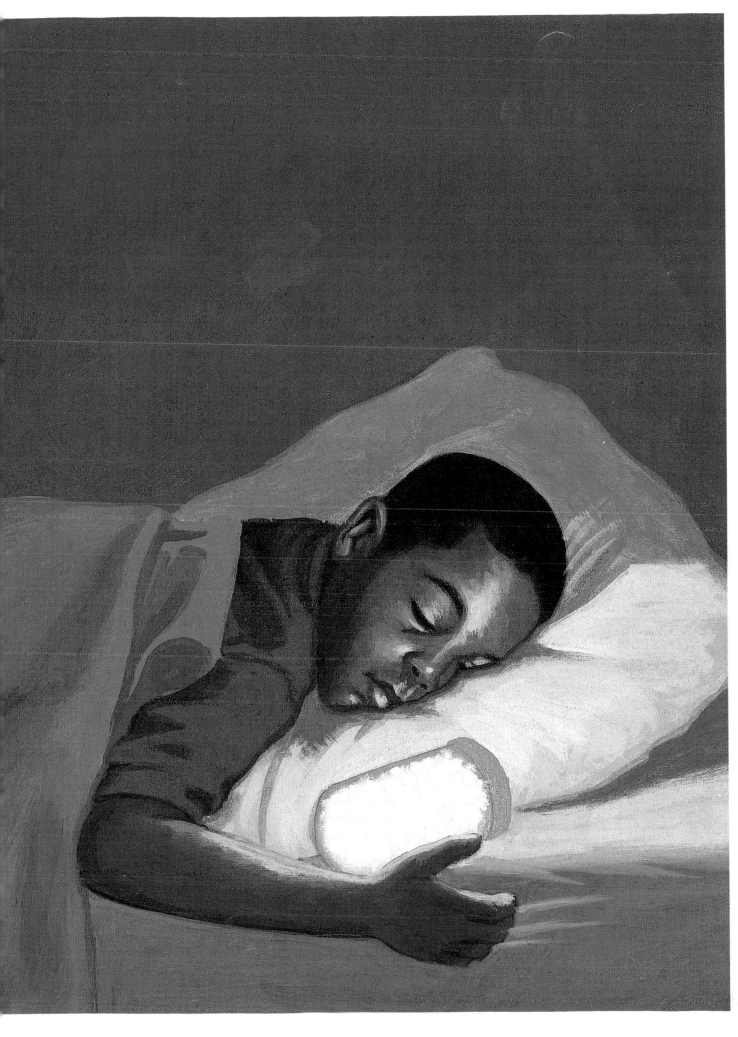